What Next, Ted?

What Next, Ted?

by Peter Kavanagh

One morning, during breakfast,
Ted heard a knock on the door.

"Good morning!" said the Wizard.
"I wonder if you'd do me a favour?"

"The Wicked Witch is causing
trouble. I have to go after her."

"Please look after Pup for me
while I'm gone," said the Wizard.

"I'd love to, Wizard," said Ted.
"You can count on me!"

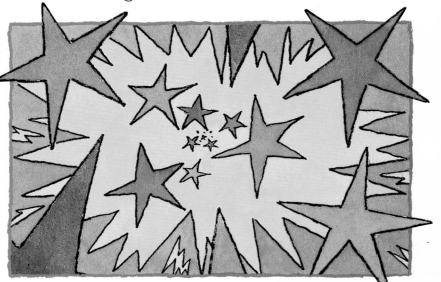

With a flash of magic, the Wizard
disappeared.

You choose what happens next!

Now follow one colour only:

Pup gets lost . . .

When the smoke cleared, Ted found that Pup was gone.

Finish breakfast . . .

"Come inside, Pup, while I finish my breakfast," said Ted.

Visit a circus . . .

"Let's go to the circus," Ted said to Pup. They set off.

Ted ran around everywhere looking for the missing little dog.

"The Wizard will be so cross with me," thought Ted.

Pup ran ahead of Ted and got to the breakfast first.

"Naughty Pup," said Ted. "There's none left for me!"

"I love the clowns," said Ted. "What do you like best, Pup?"

They watched a man juggling balls.

"I will have to run away and never come back."

Sadly, he packed a few favourite things and said goodbye to his home.

"Luckily I have some eggs I can cook," said Ted.

But when Ted's back was turned, Pup ate the eggs as well.

And some acrobats performing clever balancing tricks.

Then a lady came out with some dancing cats.

Suddenly there was a flash! The Wizard and Pup appeared.

"Pup followed me," said the Wizard. "Hang on to him this time, Ted!"

"I hope you're full now," said Ted, "because there's nothing else to eat."

"Let's go," he said, "and find something for me to eat!"

It was terrible. Pup chased the cats and Ted chased Pup.

"I'm sorry about the dog," said Ted. "He was just playing."

You choose what happens next!

Now follow one colour only:

Visit Ted's friend, Jim . . .

Ted knocked on Jim's door.
"I'm just having breakfast," said Jim.

Go to the bun shop . . .

Ted bumped into his friend, Jim, outside the bun shop.

Pup runs away . . .

Ted put Pup's lead on but Pup still ran away.

"I've had a terrible morning with that dog," moaned Ted.

"That's Pup, the Wizard's dog, isn't it?" said Jim.

Crash! Buns flew everywhere.

Jim loved buns. So did Pup.

They crashed into the apple seller and apples rolled everywhere.

They knocked down a display of pots outside a shop.

Pup ran ahead and was eating Jim's breakfast.

"Naughty dog," said Jim. "Don't eat my breakfast."

In no time at all Pup had eaten the buns. There were none left for Jim.

"The Wizard's dog is making my buns disappear fast!" said Jim.

They tripped up an ice-cream seller by the fountain.

Ted's friend, Jim, caught Pup outside the park.

"Do you have any more food?"
asked Ted, "I'm quite hungry, too!"

"Not you as well!" said Jim.
"Well, Pup, at least he asked first."

"He is such a naughty pup," said
Ted. "I'm trying to look after him."

"Well, you're not doing a very good
job of it, are you?" said Jim.

"Hello, Ted," said Jim. "What's
going on?"

"Oh, nothing," said Ted. "I'm just
taking this dog for a walk."

You choose what happens next!

Now follow one colour only:

Visit the Wizard's house . . .

"I'm off to see the Wizard," said Jim.

Have a balloon ride . . .

"Oh, look, Ted! It's a balloon race," said Jim.

Follow Pup's nose . . .

"Pup can smell something," said Ted. "Let's follow him."

"You can't," said Ted. "He's gone to sort out the Wicked Witch."

"Oh no!" said Jim. "It's a trap! I was going to warn him."

"Pup! What are you doing?" said Ted. "Jim, help!"

"We'll be all right as long as Pup holds on," said Jim.

"Is that a magic dog?" asked Jim.

"Oh, yes," said Ted. "He's incredibly clever!"

"He specially asked me to look after his dog," said Ted.

"We must go after him," said Jim. "We must rescue the Wizard!"

"Good dog, Pup," said Ted. "Hang on tight!"

"Woof!" said Pup and they began to fall.

"What sort of magic can he do?" asked Jim.

"He . . . er . . . well . . . um . . . finds things," said Ted.

"Rescue the Wizard? What are you talking about, Jim?" asked Ted.

"We'll have to borrow the Wizard's magic horse," said Jim.

"I think this story is finished now," said Ted.

"Quick!" said Jim. "Go back and choose another colour to follow!"

"Like horses?" asked Jim.
"Special horses," said Ted.

"Jump on," said the horses.
"We've been looking for you."

You choose which horse to ride!

Now follow one colour only:

The great white horse . . .

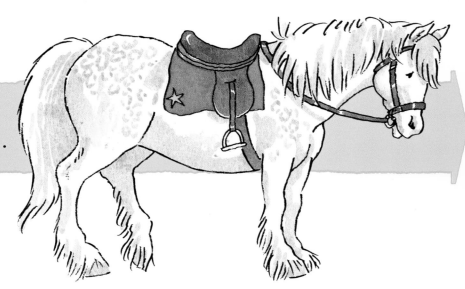

The mysterious black horse . . .

The little brown pony . . .

The great white horse took off at incredible speed.

The three friends held on as the white horse raced forwards.

The mysterious black horse turned to look at them.

"Hang on tight," he said, "I'll take you to the Wizard."

Ted, Jim and Pup leapt on to the little brown pony.

The pony didn't move. "Giddy up!" shouted Ted.

The ground became a blur as they took off. They rode across the sky.

Soon they saw a black tower reaching up through the clouds.

The horse galloped through the town and leapt into a wishing well.

They fell so fast that Ted and Jim didn't even have time to scream!

"Please stop kicking me," said the pony. "We have arrived."

With a gasp, Jim and Ted found that they were outside a castle.

"This is the Witch's castle," said Jim.
"The Wizard is in big trouble!"

The horse set them down before
three strange doors.

They landed with a bump and found
that the horse was gone.

"We must be quick!" said Jim.
"The Wizard needs our help."

"This castle belongs to the Wicked
Witch!" said Jim.

"The Wizard needs your assistance,"
said the little brown pony.

You choose which door to open!

THE BIG IRON DOOR that leads to the dark, dark corridor . . .

THE GREAT OAK DOOR that leads to the wet, dripping tunnel . . .

Now follow one colour only:

THE NARROW ARCHED DOOR that leads to the steep spiral stairs . . .

Pup led them down a dark, dark corridor, growling as he went.

Suddenly a trapdoor opened and the floor disappeared beneath them.

The roof was so low that Ted and Jim had to crawl through the tunnel.

"We must help the Wizard escape from the Wicked Witch!" said Jim.

Inside they found stone stairs spiralling downwards.

They could hear the cackling laughter of the Wicked Witch.

With a crash, they slid down into a cage with iron bars.

There was a shriek of laughter in the dark. The Wicked Witch appeared.

"But how can two small friends help a mighty Wizard?" asked Ted.

"You can't!" cried the Wicked Witch, with a cackling laugh.

"The Wizard must be in big trouble," whispered Jim.

A moment later they gasped. The Wizard was in the Witch's cauldron!

"What have we here?" she laughed.
"More wizards caught in my trap?"

"We chose the wrong door," said
Ted. "Go back and choose another!"

With a flash of magic, she turned
Ted and Jim into a couple of frogs.

"Wrong door!" croaked Jim. "Hop
back and try again!"

"I'm going to boil you into a magic
potion!" cackled the Witch.

"You always were a terrible cook,"
said the Wizard.

You choose what happens in the end!

Now follow one colour only:

Pup to the rescue . . .

"Nobody can save you now, Wizard!" shrieked the Wicked Witch.

The Witch's Cat . . .

"Trapped by my cat on your hat!" laughed the Wicked Witch.

Wizard Stew . . .

"Now where's my favourite cook book?" said the Witch.

"Except myself," said Pup in the Wizard's voice.

"Woof!" said the Wizard in the bubbling cauldron.

Without his hat the Wizard couldn't work his magic.

Instead he whistled, twice.

"Oh no!" said the Wizard. "Not the dreaded book of nasty recipes!"

"Here we are . . ." said the Witch. "How to stew wizards . . ."

There was a flash of magic and the Wicked Witch was turned to stone.

The Wizard changed back into himself again.

Pup charged in, growling fiercely. The cat screeched and ran away.

The magic hat flew safely back to the Wizard.

At that moment Pup bit the Witch on the leg.

"Ow!" she screamed and jumped backwards into her cook books.

He changed Pup back into a dog and rescued him from the cauldron.

"Come along, my brave friends," he said, "it's time to go home."

"Curses!" cried the Witch, disappearing in a cloud of smoke.

"So, the Witch's trap was a cat on your magic hat," said Jim.

With a mighty, dusty crash, the books buried the Wicked Witch.

"Well done, Pup," said the Wizard. "Help me out please, friends."

"You knew about the Witch's trap!" said Jim.

"So you changed places with Pup!" said Ted. The Wizard smiled.

"That's right," said the Wizard. "But I had something better."

"What's that?" said Ted. "Good friends," said the Wizard.

"Wizard Stew – how disgusting," said Ted.

"I'm sure it would have been delicious," said the Wizard.

For Jim, the brother
P.K.

Scholastic Children's Books
Commonwealth House, 1-19 New Oxford Street
London WC1A 1NU, UK
a division of Scholastic Ltd

London – New York – Toronto – Sydney – Auckland
Mexico City – New Delhi – Hong Kong

First published in hardback in the UK by Scholastic Ltd, 2001
This paperback edition published by Scholastic Ltd, 2002

Text and illustrations copyright © Peter Kavanagh 2001

ISBN 0 439 97900 5

Printed and bound in Belgium

2 4 6 8 10 9 7 5 3 1

The right of Peter Kavanagh to be identified as the author and illustrator of this work has been asserted
by him in accordance with the Copyright, Designs and Patents Act, 1988.